Angels Among The Lakes

Other titles by Sarah Foster
(Previously Sarah Schultz or Schwersenska)

Between the Lines
In Your Face Erotica
The Ultimate Art of Erotica
Generations of Cooking

Angels Among The Lakes

By

Sarah Foster

Printed electronically in the United States of America 2004

ISBN-13: 978-1-946205-03-2 Crystal Dreams Publishing

ISBN-13: 9781413720730 in Print 2004 by Publish America

Ladies of the Lakes Publishing LLC

2022 Print Version – ISBN 13 – 978-1-946205-31-5

Ladies of the Lakes Publishing LLC
1725 Cindy Street
Ishpeming, MI 49849

www.ladiesofthelakespub.com

Ladies
of the
Lakes
Publishing

2004 Dedication:

Morris Striplin (Strip)
for pushing me on to get this book done back
then. And for being my very first published author,
believing in the bigger picture.

2019 Addition:
Thank you to my daughter, Heather-Lee, my
peanut,
for putting up with my trashy books
and being the creative person
behind our company.
Love you lil peanut

And my Woogy.
Thank God for mighty cables.
I love you to the ends of the earth.
And then to Ish.

CHAPTER 1

Gabrielle looked around nervously as she lifted the skirt of her white silk gown and stepped into the lake. She shivered at the coolness of the water on her feet and on her legs, and then she sighed. The water felt so good. Holding her breath, she plunged into the deep water and came up gasping for air a few moments later. The water below was even colder, little waves touching her nipples, making them fully erect, and seeping into her regions below.

That was all she needed: a quick, refreshing dive. She turned and walked toward shore, looking around again to make sure no one would see her getting out in her soaked gown. Seeing no one about, she walked up onto the shore, picked up her towel and started drying her long golden hair. It was about noon and the sun was high, making her dark golden blonde hair shine like the most beautifully spun gold. The roundness and fullness of her nipples was visible right through her gown, and her mound of hair below stood right out as she dried her hair quickly. She had no idea that the knight watching her from the trees just beyond where she stood was already getting aroused.

He was almost unable to stand it. He wanted to take her right there, lay her down on the ground and make beautiful, sweet, passionate love to her. He couldn't get enough of her beautiful breasts, her gorgeous naked body. He was dying; he had to talk to her. He watched, entranced as she tilted her head back to dry the length of her hair. It nearly touched her round, voluptuous bottom, which he could see right through her gown. She was an angel, and he wanted to make her fly.

He decided that he had to talk to her, apologize

for stumbling upon her in this state. He walked forward until he got to the edge of the clearing where she stood. With the towel on her head, she had not heard his approach. She was just about to start drying the rest of her body when he cleared his throat to announce his presence, startling her nearly back into the lake.

"My Lord! Do you always sneak up on people like that? How long have you been standing there? Have you been watching me?" Gabrielle had fire in her eyes and fury in her voice. She was spewing out questions left and right, not giving the gentle knight a chance to explain his rudeness. She barely remembered to cover herself with her small towel.

"My Lady, if you will forgive me, I did not see you nor hear you, as I was traveling. I have only just stumbled upon you. I do apologize. I did not mean to startle you. Please forgive me."

Gabrielle could not say anything for a moment, as she was mesmerized by the stranger's beautiful green eyes. They sparkled against his reddish-blonde hair, which was down to his shoulders, matching the length of his beard. He looked scruffy and dangerous, but for some reason she found it quite attractive. He was like a giant golden angel; he fairly seemed to glow. At the same time, he was quite intimidating, standing nearly seven feet tall and built like nothing she had ever seen; he appeared to have muscles everywhere. She caught herself staring and quickly turned away.

"As long as you are more careful from now on," she finally spoke. "What are you doing in these parts of the woods, anyhow? These woods belong to the King. Are you trespassing? The guards shall be along now anytime if you are. They are not far from here, you know."

"I beg your pardon, my Lady. How rude of me. My name is Lord Byron. I do not believe we have met." *Lord Byron*, Gabrielle thought, *the friend of my father's? How delightful!* She extended her hand to him slowly, still a bit leery. He gently held it for a moment before brushing his lips ever so lightly across her skin. When contact was made, a jolt of something electric went through her body. She pulled her hand away, refusing to believe that this man could make her feel so wonderful. He had the most angelic smile. She could not believe a man of his stature could be so gentle.

"You still did not answer me," Gabrielle demanded. "Why are you in the King's woods?"

Lord Byron replied, "And you, my Lady, did not give me the pleasure of knowing your name." He kept smiling at her and she realized that he was correct -- she had simply been too mesmerized to properly introduce herself.

"I am sorry. My name is Gabrielle. How do you do?" Gabrielle curtsied appropriately, not noticing that Lord Byron looked a little taken back. Could his luck possibly be this good?

"Are you *Princess* Gabrielle, the only daughter of King Mathew?" he asked, trying to mask his delight.

Gabrielle suddenly realized she could be in real danger from this man. What if this stranger intended to kidnap her for ransom from the King? "Why do you want to know?" she snapped.

Sensing the panic in her voice put him immediately at ease. He threw his head back, tossing back all of his lovely hair and roared a deep, powerful laugh. "My Lady, please, do not be afraid. I am on my way to see your father now. I am not in any way here to harm you. I do apologize if my nature made it seem so." He saw her calm down a little and blush sheepishly.

"Might I escort you back to the castle, Princess?" He knew he was being a bit forward and casual with her, but he wanted to see just how far he could go.

"Please, call me Gabrielle. I do not feel like being a Princess right at this moment. My father and I are not on good terms right now, not that it is any of your business. I suppose, you can lead me home. But 'Gabrielle' will be just fine, thank you, Lord Byron." He was touched at her honesty and politeness. He had heard that she was a bit of a handful when she wanted to be -- but she was a damn beautiful one at that.

Gazing the length of her gown, he couldn't help taking in every curve of her legs, her buttocks, her waist, her voluptuous breasts, her erect nipples and . . . her blushing face as she caught his gaze. He cleared his throat again and looked away, trying not to smile.

"Is there something you find amusing about this, my Lord? I do not have anything else to put on right now, thanks to your presence." He could tell she was getting angry.

"No, my Lady. It is just that you are so beautiful, I could not help myself." He realized that was the wrong thing to say, a moment too late. Her face went red with rage.

"*Help yourself*?! Do you think you can just *help yourself*? Would you prefer it if I just stood here while you had a good look?" She was yelling now; her face was turning scarlet. He had to laugh; even as angry as she was, she was simply delightful. Her brown eyes lit up her face when she was angry. His laughing made her even madder and she walked up to him with her hand clenched into a fist. She pulled back and tried to hit his chest, but he caught her fragile, delicate wrist easily in his strong hand. He stared into her beautiful, wild eyes. She stared right back.

"How dare you mock me," she said quietly. His

body heat was radiating, making her wet and aroused. She tried to tell herself this was not the way it was supposed to be. He could not break his gaze from hers. Her lips were full and anticipating, her face was so perfect, and her hair, her mouth . . . he could not take it any longer. Keeping her wrist held fast, he gripped the small of her back with his other hand and kissed her. He held her so close; she could not get away no matter how she tried.

She struggled against him, fighting with her free hand, pounding on his shoulders, her verbal protests muffled by his mouth closing in on hers. What was this barbarian doing? She could not move. His powerful grasp kept her locked into place. His mouth was so hot and inviting against hers. Her legs went numb, and her arms started to tingle. His eager lips gently pried hers open, and finally she responded.

Their tongues danced in each other's mouths, their bodies pressed against each other. She felt him harden against her and noticed just how wet she had become. Her arms stopped struggling and started pulling him closer. His hand went to the back of her head and held her there. Both of her arms were free now, but she did not try to run anymore. His hand fell from her back down onto her nearly bare buttocks, grabbing them firmly. She moaned involuntarily, not even realizing how turned on she was. His hand stroked her breast so gently. It was as if a feather had touched her. She could not believe how delicate this man could be.

He was not hurting her, nor forcing her; she was free to run if she wanted to. She knew that now, but she had no desire to flee. His hands, huge and strong yet so soft and smooth, were suddenly under her gown, warm and tender against her cool skin. He felt her shiver and pulled her even closer, instinctively protecting her and making her feel safe. His manly fingers moved inside her and marveled at how very turned on she really was. She moaned again, gasping for air; he was driving her crazy. This man, this strange knight from out of nowhere, was pushing her most intimate buttons – something no other man had ever done before.

He quickly guided her to the ground, to a blanket Gabrielle hadn't noticed before. *Had he planned this all along?* She briefly wondered, before dismissing the idea. He was out of his armor before she knew it and lying on top of her. It seemed impossible, yet she was not being crushed underneath him. She felt very calm and comfortable in this position, and found herself wanting him more than ever. His heat, his flesh, was driving her to the edge, and nothing else seemed to matter.

He began kissing her neck and she shivered again. Her whole body was shaking. Before it was too late, she leaned up and whispered into his ear that it was her first time. He was amazed – and honored – that she would let a man like him take such a sacred thing way from her. Touched, he promised to be gentle as he moved closer.

She felt him touch her, just the head at first; teasing to make sure she was ready. Then he started to slide in. She gritted her teeth as a white hot pain shot through her lower regions, but in a few seconds the pain was gone and she felt slightly numbed. *My Lord*, she thought, *if this is what it is, I don't want any part of it*. But it wasn't.

He started moving in a rhythm so gentle, it was almost hypnotic. Sliding in and out of her, it felt so right and she melted underneath him. His hands were wrapped around her, one on each side of her buttocks. He started moving faster and faster. She could not believe the feeling rushing through her body. She couldn't help but moan loudly. *Oh yes*, she thought, *this feels so right*. Suddenly a wave of electricity shot through her whole body. It felt amazing but she didn't have the slightest idea of what was going on and could only grip him tightly with her arms as her legs and thighs spasmed wildly. When it was finally done, she realized what had happened. She realized that they had gone together, and she smiled. He sank into her neck, kissing her passionately.

"You, my Lady, are an angel," he whispered heavily. "I cannot believe I have found a creature so pure and so delicate." He looked into her eyes and decided that she was to be his woman. No other man would ever touch her; no other man would as much as look at her ever again. He would get the King's permission and make her his wife. But he could not tell her this now. He was already late for his meeting with the King.

Wordlessly, he helped Gabrielle to her feet and she set about making herself look presentable to her father, the King, even after her swim in the lake. She kept stealing glances at him. What was she thinking? Why was she looking at him so? He wondered to himself. He decided there was no need to waste time – he would learn and love everything about her by the end of the week. When she was ready to go, he offered his arm and together they started on the journey back to the castle.

Gabrielle remained silent for a bit, although a hundred thoughts were running through her head. Was this man for real? How could he just come in and sweep her off her feet like this? It did not seem at all possible. How could she permit herself to be broken in by such a beastly thing? Thinking about it suddenly made her feel very dirty and ashamed. But his eyes, the color of sparkling emeralds; his hands, his touch, the feeling when he was inside her . . .

She started to get flushed again and immediately dismissed her thoughts. She was angry at him now, for making her feel this way. Who in the bloody hell did he think he was? They soon came to a clearing where four men and five horses waited expectantly. The men were standing around talking while the horses grazed contentedly. Then Gabrielle noticed one of the horses, a powerful white stallion, looked up and started walking straight toward Lord Byron. She quickly put the pieces together: these were his men, and his horse. Her face grew red and she dropped his arm immediately.

"You came all that way to watch me and bring me back here while they awaited you? You inconsiderate, lying bastard!" she fumed. "How dare you! Who do you think you are?!" Gabrielle started kicking and punching Lord Byron, but he grabbed her arms and held her against him tight. He was shocked at her use of such harsh language and her sudden hostility.

"My Lady, please, let me explain."

"I will do no such thing! You wait until I tell my father! You will be hung, do you hear me?!" Gabrielle was crying now and all her energy had gone. She had given herself up to a man who had planned on taking her from the beginning. She felt so disgusted with herself. She leaned against Lord Byron and wept, not realizing he was comforting her ever so gently, stroking her silken hair. He spoke to her calmly, in a whisper only she could hear:

"My Lady Gabrielle, your father sent us looking for you. He needed you back at the castle. I heard you in the water so I had the men stay here, for fear you were, well, without your garments on. I am sorry if you misunderstood, my Lady. I did not mean to disrespect you in any way. I was not aware of who you even were until you told me. I could never hurt you, Gabrielle. Know that now and do not ever doubt me again. Is that understood?"

Gabrielle looked at him, her anger dissipating, and nodded her head. She could not believe how authoritative he was being with her, but she listened and, for some reason, she believed him. He climbed up on his horse, then lifted her up and set her gently on his lap. She leaned against his chest and sat there quietly all the way home, ashamed that she had made such a fool of herself in front of Byron's men.

When they reached the bridge just before the castle door, Gabrielle asked to be let off. Byron helped her down carefully, then dismounted himself and stood at her side. Gabrielle looked at the men as they stared at her and Byron expectantly. Byron made the first move to break the awkward silence.

"Gabrielle, please do not be afraid of these men; they will protect you. Allow me to introduce my finest and most trustworthy companions: Del, Eric, Aaron, and Sebastian." Gabrielle nodded at each of them as Byron said their names. They, in turn, graciously bid her a good day and smiled. She felt at ease with the way they were all so nice to her. Byron turned to Gabrielle and again offered his arm. "Now then, let's go tend to your father, shall we?"

CHAPTER 2

Gabrielle felt weak and confused as she and Lord Byron walked across the bridge and to her father's castle door. Byron held the door open for Gabrielle as she led the way inside, followed by Byron and his men. Immediately her maid, Sheila, came and took her towel and asked Gabrielle if she would like to get cleaned up for dinner. Gabrielle nodded and said she would be up shortly. She heard her father's voice in the next room and quickly left the group to confront her father. The King heard his beautiful daughter approaching and smiled warmly.

"Gabby, my angel, how was your swim?"

"Father! How dare you send strange men out to find me while I am swimming in my private lake! Do you not know what the word *private* means? Lord Byron practically saw me with nothing on! Do you know how embarrassed I was? And don't call me 'Gabby'! I don't like it! I am not a little girl anymore!"

"Do you always talk to your father that way, Gabrielle?" Lord Byron interrupted as he walked in the room. "I am sure he meant no harm sending me for you." To Gabrielle's surprise, King Mathew quickly dismissed Gabrielle and turned his attention to Byron.

"There you are old chap! How have you been? Thank you for collecting Gabrielle for me. I am sorry if she got a bit out of hand for you."

"Nonsense, Mathew. It was my pleasure to escort your daughter home. She was a complete angel. I would be honored to do it anytime, Sire." He winked knowingly at Gabrielle, but she was in no mood for his jokes. How dare her father dismiss her for this man? And who was he to talk to her father so informally? Everyone addressed her father as King Mathew. The King and Byron had moved to talking about business, so she decided to go clean up for dinner.

She quietly excused herself and started walking out of the room. Her father was rambling away about something on the other side of the room, looking out the window, when Byron grabbed her and kissed her forcefully right where she stood. Her eyes went wide and she tried to pull away without making any sounds, but she could not compete with Byron's strength. Her knees were going weak again, as his tongue swept her mouth. Her nipples grew erect under her still damp gown. He broke the kiss and drew his head back so he could look at her clearly. There was no amusement in his eyes now, only tenderness and sincere caring. He dropped his hands and placed then gently on her waist, feeling her bareness underneath. She turned quickly and ran out of the room. Byron sighed and smiled. She would be his, he was sure of it.

"Lord Byron? Have you heard anything I have said? You look as if you are off in a dream world. Is there something wrong?" The King was amused by Lord Byron's lack of attention.

"No, King Mathew, nothing is wrong at all. I was thinking about your Gabrielle, actually. She is quite a little lady." The King was not surprised. He nodded in agreement.

"Ahh, yes. My dear, sweet Gabby. Her temper gets out of control every now and then since her mother passed away. She has her mother's spirit and determination, that is for sure. You would make a good husband for her, Lord Byron. Why don't you take the girl under your wing and put a saddle on my wild little filly?"

Lord Byron chuckled at the thought: him, taming the King's daughter, when his temper was no better than hers. Maybe that was why they would be perfect together – at least they had something in common. The King had a great sense of humor.

"Is something funny, Byron? I am serious. That would be just the thing to get the girl out of here when King Louis comes here with his boys next week. Those lads are nothing but trouble, and I don't want them anywhere near my Gabby. Would you do me the honor of looking after her a fortnight and keeping her safe? I would compensate you well." Lord Byron could not believe his luck. How very ironic.

"Nonsense. You won't pay me one coin. I would be happy to watch your daughter for you, Sire. I know the boys you speak of and you are right, they are no match for your daughter. I will have to put up with her 'wild streak' for a couple of weeks, but it cannot be any worse than some of my men."

The King rolled his eyes. "Oh, Lord Byron, if you only knew my Gabrielle, if you only knew . . ." The men laughed and walked into the dining hall together.

King Mathew, Princess Gabrielle, Lord Byron and his men were all seated at the large table that ran the length of the dining room a few moments later when the King shared his plans with his daughter. Her reaction was less than pleased. "Have you absolutely lost it, Father?" she screamed. "No way am I going to spend two weeks with this . . . this . . . *barbarian*! I will not! I refuse!" Gabrielle turned her head to the wall and folded her arms across her chest. Her father rolled his eyes and Byron chuckled under his breath. The King was in his usual chair at the head of the table, with his daughter to his side and Lord Byron across from her. The men were all seated next to him.

"Gabrielle, please. I do not want you around here when King Louis comes around with his deviants. I will not have it. Just go and get to know Lord Byron – he is a rather charming person." The King smirked and winked knowingly at Lord Byron.

"Father, do you think this amusing? I am not going and that is my final word, do you hear me?" Gabrielle slammed her hand down on the table and the room went quiet. King Mathew looked up at her with a stern face.

"Young lady, you will go with Lord Byron tonight, and that is my final word. I do not want to hear you raise your voice to me like that again. You are not too big to take over my knee, Gabrielle. Now, no more talk of this. You are leaving tonight and that is final!" The King's face was red. He started eating hungrily, not looking up from his plate. Gabrielle had her face down, feeling ashamed for yelling at her father and making a fool of herself.

"Yes, Father. I am sorry. Please excuse me." She got up and ran into the library. The men never said a word, just kept on eating. Lord Byron excused himself and followed Gabrielle, telling the King he would talk to the girl.

Opening the large oak doors to the library, Byron was in awe of the stately room. There were literally thousands of leather-bound books, along with a massive desk and comfortable, inviting furniture placed throughout the spacious area. Gabrielle was sitting in the far corner on a chair, looking out the window. She heard him close the door after he entered, but kept her gaze to the window as she spoke.

"You can leave. I do not need anyone to mock me. You got your way, now leave me alone."

"Gabrielle, it was your father's request, not mine. Do not be angry with me. We will have fun these next two weeks, you will see." Gabrielle stood and walked right up to him. He was so tall; she had to practically look straight upward to see him.

"Have *fun* with you? After what you did to me? Why, that is simply--" Lord Byron grabbed her arm and pulled her tight, wrapping his other arm around her waist.

"What I did to you? My Lady, you were just as consenting, if I remember correctly. Are you denying that you liked what we shared?" He looked at her with hard eyes, yet they were as full of tenderness and passion as they were every time she looked at him. He demanded an answer, and she could not lie to him. She began to put her head down but he tilted her chin back up.

"No, Lord Byron. I do not deny it."

"And do you deny you have feelings for me?"

"What? Are you just as mad as my father? How can I have feelings for a man I have only just met?"

"So, you deny it, then?" Lord Byron smiled at her. She was melting. She wanted him so badly, but she could not show her weakness.

"No, I do not completely deny it, but that gives you no right to . . ." Before she could finish, Lord Byron kissed her hard and full, his tongue magically dancing in her mouth. Her breasts pressed against him, her hands went to his and she found herself returning his kiss just as deeply. She wanted him inside her again. He made her feel like a new person.

Grabbing her from behind, he picked her up and carried her over to the desk by the window. He gently pulled her gown up and felt her milky white thighs, her silky smooth skin. She inhaled deeply at his touch. He made her tremble with desire. His fingers touched lightly against her moistness, just brushing her mound of hair lightly but still sending shock waves through her.

Before she knew it, he had pulled out his

already hardened manhood and entered her. She gasped and started to moan loudly, but he covered her mouth so the men in the next room wouldn't hear. He kept his hand firmly over her mouth while he pumped into her, back and forth. Her hands were spread out behind her, bracing herself, as he held the small of her back and drove into her hungrily. She was irritated at first that he would cover her mouth, but then found it simply erotic. She thrust her hips to meet him as he let out a moan, kissing her neck, her shoulders, her breasts. She felt that surging feeling once again, the same one she felt in the woods, and she screamed underneath his hand. He held her tight as his orgasm met hers and they shared yet another wonderful experience together.

When they had both caught their breath, he helped her clean up and get herself back in order. She looked at him cautiously, not really knowing what to say. He held her face in his hands and kissed her lovingly.

"I will have you, Gabrielle. I want you to be with me forever. Know this now, as I will not argue with you about it. You are mine and someday, you will be my wife." He kissed her again, leaving her jaw agape as if she had just been slapped in the face.

"You will *have* me? Just who do you think you are? You have no right to tell me whom I shall marry, where I shall be, or anything else! You ignorant man! Get out of here! I do not want to ever see you again! Get out of my sight!" Furious, Gabrielle started throwing books at him left and right. Lord Byron thought it was a good chance to make a safe escape back to the dining room. He smiled widely at her and left the library.

When he returned to the table, the King and his men were all laughing, for they had heard Gabrielle yelling. Lord Byron returned to his seat, laughing as well and agreeing with the King that his daughter could use some real taming.

In the library, Gabrielle sat back down with a submissive sigh. She hated that man, but she knew he was right: she was falling in love with him. She knew he would have her, and she knew she would gladly let him. She could easily give in to it and let her true feelings show, but that would make her seem weak. Oh, what should she do? Tired from all the fighting, she lay down on the couch and drifted off into a deep sleep.

By the time the men were finished in the dining room a few hours later, Sheila had Gabrielle's bags packed and ready to go. Lord Byron had Del and Eric carry the Princess' things to the waiting horses. The King had provided one of his very best horses for Gabrielle. They packed it with only her things, as Lord Byron wanted her to ride in his lap so she could continue to sleep. When all of their things were packed, Sebastian and Byron went to the library to gather the slumbering princess.

With Sebastian holding open the heavy library doors, Lord Byron walked over to the couch to fetch the sleeping beauty. He looked down at her and couldn't help but smile. She slept so peacefully. He could see her breasts rising and falling to the rhythm of her slumber. Her hair was spread out like beautiful angel's wings. He bent down and gently placed his arms underneath her to pick her up. While lifting her gently, her gown was pulled down a bit in front and one of her breasts was partially exposed. It looked so soft, so pure. He put his lips to hers and kissed her gently. He was startled when she kissed him back.

"My Lord, where on earth are you taking me?" Gabrielle looked sleepily up to him.

"Hush now, my Princess. You sleep. Tonight, we will ride to my neck of the woods. Go back to sleep now." He kissed her again as her eyes closed.

"All right, my love, whatever you say," she sleepily whispered before she drifted back off. Lord Byron could not help but smile. She had called him her love.

"I don't mean to break up the party, Romeo, but we have to get going," Sebastian called from the door. Byron cleared his throat and tried to look serious. He carried the sleeping Gabrielle swiftly through the great halls and outside to where the other men, along with King Mathew, were waiting. When they had mounted up and were ready to go, the King kissed his daughter and insisted they not wake her, for he had no patience to argue with her any more that night. They bid farewell to the King and started out on their journey, with Gabrielle riding securely and comfortably in Lord Byron's strong arms.

CHAPTER 3

Gabrielle awoke to the sound of laughter. She stretched and sat up, realizing she was on the ground, sitting on one blanket and covered with another. Del, Eric, Aaron and Sebastian were all sitting around a campfire laughing heartily. She did not see Lord Byron anywhere. She stood up and self-consciously tried to straighten her hair out as best she could.

"There is no need to do that around us, Princess Gabrielle. You are always beautiful in our eyes," Sebastian said rather bashfully. She saw him blush and quickly turn back to the fire while the others picked on him for being so sentimental.

"Why, thank you, Sebastian. How very sweet of you," she replied as she walked over to the fire. The men moved around to make room for her, but before she sat down she started looking around for Byron.

"Our Lord is down by the lake, my Lady," Del offered. "He usually likes to go for a morning swim." She paused and looked at them all with a mischievous grin on her face. She turned and started to walk towards the lake when Eric came after her.

"My Lady, I don't mean to be rude, but our Lord, he is . . . well, probably without clothing if he is still swimming. I'm not so sure you would want to go down there."

"Is he, now? Well, let's just see how he likes it." She started off and could hear the men behind her laughing. She didn't care. Lord Byron had spied upon her while she was enjoying her morning swim, and now it was her turn for revenge. She never did look at him very closely without his clothes on, other than his face.

A few moments later she came to a clearing by

the shore and saw a pile of clothes near a tree by the water. She smiled to herself, satisfied that Byron was still in the water and presumably nude. She looked around in the lake, however, and could not find him anywhere. The water looked simply inviting, but when she heard the splashing she ran and hid behind a very large oak tree just as Byron slowly emerged from under the water.

His body was glistening in the sun. It was like he was sent from heaven; he was positively glowing. He was heading toward shore when she realized she was stuck there, behind that tree. *Damn*, she thought. *What if he sees me*? He started to walk up onto shore and even though she turned her head to keep from making eye contact, she had the feeling he knew she was there. She was a bit embarrassed, but since he didn't say anything or act any differently, she turned back to watch him anyway.

Her jaw dropped at the sight of this burly man. He was raw muscle. Every muscle rippled as he dried himself off. She tried to pull herself together but was already getting all hot below. *What a gorgeous man*, she thought. He lifted the towel to dry his beautiful hair and exposed his most exquisite muscle. She gasped and quickly put a hand over her mouth, but couldn't help staring in awe. *Is that what was in me*? She wondered to herself. *It is simply huge*! Her breasts were swollen, as was her clitoris. She wanted to be touched so badly. She dared not move. Lord Byron got dressed and headed back toward the others.

When she thought he was out of sight, Gabrielle leaned back and sighed. *That was too close*, she told herself. She walked carefully out from behind the tree, removed her gown and quickly slipped into the water. She needed to cool down and fast. She dove under, submerging every inch of herself in the soothing coolness of the lake. When she came up for air, Byron was standing directly in front of her, again completely nude. She gasped in surprise and tried to cover herself.

"How nice of you to join me here this morning, Princess." He had a cocky grin on his face. She blushed and tried to hide, but there was nowhere else to go.

"I ...I was just going for a morning swim. I did not see you here. I am sorry; I can leave if you like." Gabrielle tried to walk past him but he grabbed her arm and would not let her go.

"Nonsense, Gabrielle. You know better. I would love to have you stay here with me. It is strange that you did not know I was here, though. I could have sworn I was in plain view from behind that tree."

Gabrielle's face went bright scarlet as she searched for a way to explain herself. "I, um, well, I was waiting--"

Byron interrupted with a hearty laugh. "It is quite all right, my darling. I did not mind that you watched me. In fact, I found it quite erotic. Did you like what you saw?" He knew he was putting her on the spot, but he wanted to know how she felt.

"Um . . . Lord, I am so embarrassed." She put her face in her hands to hide her shame. Byron pulled her closer to him. Her nipples touched him, sending electricity through both of them. She instantly got wet again. She wanted him to just hold her there. She liked being this close to him.

Byron tilted his head down and rested his chin on her head. She smelled wonderful. He took her in and wrapped his giant arms around her. He was growing hard and she could already feel him stiffen in front of her, pressing against her. He walked her farther out into the water so it was up to his chest, then he picked her up. She slid down gently onto his rock hard cock; it was so much easier in the water. Her hands held on tightly around his neck. She kept looking toward shore to see if the men would be there.

"Relax, my love, no one will bother us here. They know to leave us alone. Just relax," he coaxed. Trusting him, she relaxed and let him hold onto her and make her ride him. She gasped and moaned with pleasure. She loved the way he felt inside her. After a few minutes, he stopped and walked to the shore, Gabrielle still holding on to him tightly. When they were out of the water, he gently lay her down on the sand. She questioned his movements, wondering why he had stopped, but quickly saw his intentions when he knelt in front of her.

"My Lord . . ." she half-heartedly argued as she began to push him away, but she was powerless against him as he leaned into her and placed his tongue right inside her. Her hips nearly flew a foot off the ground. She had never felt anything like it before. He held her down and kept licking her most private areas. Her eyes were rolling around in her head and she was making noises she didn't even recognize as her own. He grabbed her clitoris between his teeth and nibbled on it. She was nearly yelling in ecstasy now. His tongue darted in and out of her. He lapped the inner folds of her hot, pink flesh. She was trembling from head to toe. Her knees were weak and she could no longer feel her arms. Where did this man come from?

She felt a finger slide inside her, and then another. She was so disoriented with pleasure, she could hardly see straight. Lord Byron suddenly stopped and rolled her over. She began to protest, but quickly refrained as he grabbed her hips and pulled them up so her behind met him.

He entered her wetness with a hard thrust. She squealed and then realized she was quite loud and clamped her mouth shut. He slammed into her, back and forth, his groin hitting her ass every time they met. His balls were bouncing off of her nether regions and she was going wild. He grabbed her hair and pulled back. It hurt her, yet she found it very exciting. Her knees were starting to hurt as well, but she did not care. Lord Byron let out a low groan, as if he was being hurt, then he let one final massive thrust into her and held her there. At that same moment, Gabrielle came with him. Her whole body spasmed then went limp as shock waves rode through her. Byron still had hold of her hips and held her. She was weeping now. Not because she hurt or was sad, but because she had never experienced anything like this before. He rolled her back over and kissed her deeply.

"Good morning, my fair Lady Gabrielle." He smiled at her and then helped her up and let her get cleaned off in the lake, before getting dressed himself. When they had finished, they walked up together by the others, who were packing up the horses and getting ready to go. Gabrielle tried not to look any of the other men in the eye. She was sure they knew what she and Lord Byron had been up to.

Lord Byron helped Gabrielle on her horse, smiling sweetly at her. When he walked away to mount his own horse, Del came up quietly beside her. He gently brushed his hand over the back of her hair. She threw him a wondering glance. "What on earth are you doing, Del?"

"Sorry, my Lady. You, um, had a piece of sand in your hair. I was getting it off for you." Gabrielle blushed deeply, for she knew the others were listening.

"Oh. Thank you. It must have been from the lake." Gabrielle turned away and quickly rode her horse next to Byron's. The others chuckled and left her alone.

"How far to your place now, Lord Byron?" Gabrielle asked him.

"Please, just call me Byron. I don't call you 'Princess' Gabrielle, do I?" He winked as he continued, "Not far. Half a day's ride and we will be there. There will be room for you there to put your things and to sleep in privacy if you like. If I need to go to town, one of the men will be with you at all times."

"I do not need to be protected, Lord Byron. I am a big girl; I can handle myself, thank you." Gabrielle saw right away that she offended him and wished she could take it back.

"You will be with one of us at all times!" he repeated sternly. "I won't hear another word about it, *Princess*." He rode further ahead, intentionally putting space between them. She did not know what to even say to him. *You big ox*, she thought. Sebastian rode up on one side of her and Aaron, whom she had not yet spoken to, rode up on the other.

"He means no harm, my Lady. He just wants you to be safe," Sebastian told her.

"He's right," Aaron agreed. "There are nasty barbarians around these parts. You should not ever go out alone. You could get lost easily, or even hurt. Worse yet, one of the other Lords may find you and try to take you away."

"Take me away? Why on earth would they do such a thing?" Gabrielle thought this was all nonsense.

"Princess Gabrielle," Sebastian patiently explained, "Down here, if a Lord wants a lady, he takes her. He does not ask."

"Right," Aaron added, nodding toward Lord Byron. "Except if she belongs to another Lord."

"Are you telling me that while we are here, I belong to Lord Byron? That is utterly foolish. I have never heard such a thing. I will simply tell them—"

"Sorry, Princess Gabrielle, but you cannot just tell them. They don't listen," Sebastian said. "You will have to be with Lord Byron at all costs. If you value your own life, that is." Aaron touched her arm gently and added, "And even if you don't, I think our Lord up there does quite a bit." The two men rode off together to catch up to their boss, leaving her in the middle with Eric and Del behind her. She sighed and resigned herself to the fact that it was only for two weeks; what could possibly happen?

At that instant, a jolt of hot white pain shot through her arm and she instinctively jerked back on the reins to stop her horse. She grabbed her arm and felt the blood trickling down. Looking closer, she saw the tiny arrow sticking out of her arm and quietly gasped, "Lord Byron!"

Del rode up next to her and saw the arrow immediately. "Byron! We have company!" he bellowed. Byron turned and saw Gabrielle's arm, rage overtaking him as he realized what had happened. He hollered something Gabrielle could not understand. Her horse was moving again, being led by Eric. She saw about half a dozen other men, whom she did not recognize, coming out of the woods on foot. They were fighting! She tried to look back, but Eric was leading her away too fast. Out of the corner of her eye, she saw Byron jump off his horse and draw his sword before she fainted dead away.

CHAPTER 4

"Gabrielle? Can you hear me? Lady Gabrielle?" It was Sebastian's whispering voice she heard upon waking. She opened her eyes slowly. Her head throbbed, and her arm throbbed even more.

"Sebastian? Is that you?" She saw him smile and put a cool cloth back on her head.

"Yes, Princess Gabrielle, it is I. We were afraid we had lost you."

"Lost me? Why, it was only a tiny little arrow. I have no idea why I even fainted like that. It is not like me."

"It was a tiny arrow, but it was filled with a deadly poison that stops your heart within the hour, if you do not have the antidote. Luckily, we always have the antidote with us. You are one lucky girl. We got to you just in time."

Gabrielle started remembering the fight. She tried to sit up, but her arm would not support her. She rolled onto her good arm and pushed herself into a sitting position.

"Where is Lord Byron? Is he all right?" Sebastian could hear the panic in her voice and calmed her down.

"Lord Byron is fine, my Lady. Physically, anyhow. Not a man have I seen that can fight our Lord and walk away unharmed. He is very worried about you, though. We all thought you were gone." Sebastian helped Gabrielle up and let her walk over by Lord Byron, who had his back to all of them, looking off into the distance.

"Do you mind if I sit down next to you, my Lord?" Gabrielle said quietly. Surprised, Lord Byron jumped off the log he was sitting on and hugged Gabrielle tightly, being careful not to touch her arm. He pulled back and looked at her face. She was shocked to see that he had tears in his eyes.

"Gabrielle? Are you okay? Of course you are okay. I thought I had lost you. I was . . . well, I was not sure what I would have done."

"Byron? Are *you* okay? I am just fine, can't everyone see that? I will be okay once the wound on my arm heals. Why all the fret about it?" She knew what Sebastian had said about the poison, but she still thought they were carrying on a bit too much. Kissing his forehead, Gabrielle took him by the arm and sat down on the log with him. "We will be just fine," she said reassuringly as she put her head against his shoulder and drifted off once again into a poison-induced slumber. Lord Byron knew that the side effects of the antidote were making her so sleepy, so he carried her back to her blanket and told the men they would stay where they were camped until she was well enough to ride.

"Lord, don't you think it would be safer for her to be in your house instead of out here in the open like this? We can make it there in a couple of hours." Eric was right and Lord Byron knew it. He had been so preoccupied with his love and concern for Gabrielle, he could not think straight. He agreed and ordered his men to prepare to leave at once.

They packed up all of their things quickly and rode off, Gabrielle riding once again on Lord Byron's lap. She stayed in his strong arms all the way to his village, and still did not awaken until they got into town.

She was startled a few hours later by some children yelling and woke up slowly. She looked around and saw all of the townspeople staring at her. She suddenly felt very self-conscious sitting on Byron's lap like that, but at the same time she also felt protected. He must have sensed her discomfort, as he moved his arm up to rub her back, assuring her it would be all right.

"Byron, where are we?" Gabrielle whispered in Byron's ear.

"We are in my town, Gabrielle. These are my people. You will be safe here. You will rest here until I get back."

Gabrielle turned, wincing against the awful pain in her arm. "Get back? From where? You cannot leave me here! Where are you going?" Byron shushed her, calming her down with his quiet, calm voice.

"The boys and I need to back track and make sure none of those men from the woods followed us here. We are pretty sure they did not, but we want to be positive. The ladies here will take good care of you. We will not be gone long, I promise." Gabrielle knew it was pointless to argue with him.

At last they reached a large cabin on the other side of the little village. She assumed it was Byron's, as the men were tying up the horses and carrying her things inside. Byron jumped down off his horse and helped her down, careful not to touch her sore arm. He escorted her inside where she could sit down.

His home had all the feelings of a man's home and nothing more. She could see a giant king-sized bed, a table and chairs, a kitchenette, a dressing table, and a staircase leading up. Byron saw her eyes following the stairs and quickly moved her over to the table.

"You have no need to go upstairs. It is just for storage," he informed her. She sensed something else in his voice, but dismissed it for the time being. Just then, two ladies came in the room. Both of them were very young, about her age, and they were both very beautiful. She saw the adoring way they looked at Lord Byron, and a pang of jealousy shot through her. What was going on in her head? She was not that way!

"You called for us, Lord Byron?" The ladies both did a polite curtsey to him and awaited orders.

"Maggie and Sasha – this is Princess Gabrielle. She has been wounded with a poison dart and she is to stay here until my return, do you hear me? You two are to look out for her safety and health. I will have men posted outside."

The ladies both had a change of expression at the mention of Gabrielle's name. Although they were initially jealous of this new woman on Lord Byron's arm, they knew right away that she was to be respected. They both curtseyed to her.

"Yes, my Lord," they replied in unison.

Gabrielle started to rise. "Honestly, is all this really necessary, Lord Bryon? I can manage by myself and—"

"Please, do not argue with me, Gabrielle. This is how it will be, how it *has* to be, until I return, do you hear me?" Byron was very stern as he scolded her. She bowed her head and nodded. He kissed her lightly and bid her farewell as she sat back down.

"Sasha," he ordered on his way out, "go into the garden and fetch some Queen's Breath. It will dull the pain for quite a few hours. Keep it on hand. Also, you will need some medication in case she throws a fever. Maggie, get her some clean clothes and draw a bath so she can relax. I will return in a few days." And with that, he was gone, along with the two ladies and all of his men.

Gabrielle found herself alone. She stood up and peeked out the window. Two of the men were already positioned outside her door. She felt like a prisoner. She sighed and decided to go along with it for now. After all, she was only staying for two weeks, and it just did not pay to argue with Lord Byron. What a stubborn, arrogant man he was, much like her father.

A few hours later, when darkness fell, Gabrielle was bathed and dressed in fresh, clean garments. Sasha had wrapped her arm with the new medicine, and she was feeling much better. The ladies were staying with her until Lord Byron's return, sleeping on a makeshift bed they had fashioned on the floor, despite all of Gabrielle's objections. These people live like savages, she thought; she couldn't believe they were used to such things.

Later, when she noticed that the ladies were both asleep, Gabrielle decided to go for a little moonlight walk by herself. When she opened the door, the two guards outside immediately came to attention.

"Can we help you with something, my Lady?" one of the guards asked.

"No, I will be fine, thank you. I am just going for a stroll around the village to have a look around."

"But, Princess, Lord Byron said that you were to stay—"

"I know full well what he said," Gabrielle snapped, "but I am not a child. I will be fine. Besides, he is not here to growl at me right now, is he? I am going, and that is final." She started walking, knowing they would follow her but they would not try to stop her. Physically restraining royalty was unheard of.

"Very well," he sighed reluctantly. "My name is Christian, and this is Peter; we are at your service, my Lady," he said, as they both bowed respectfully to their charge.

Gabrielle walked along, admiring all the little hutches, shops, and the beautiful gardens. It was quite a remarkable place. She saw a path wandering off into the woods that looked as if it was used quite often. When she asked one of the guards where it led, they told her it went down to their lake. She insisted on seeing it, even though the path was dark and out of the way, so the guards reluctantly agreed to escort her there.

The lake was just as beautiful as hers back in her father's woods. There was a light fog settling on the lake, making it hard to see clear across it. She was just dying for a midnight swim, but the guards were there and they would see everything underneath her wet clothes if she did. Weighing her options, she finally smiled and decided she did not care. She ran into the lake and dove under the dark water, barely hearing the guards protesting in the background.

Gabrielle paddled about, playing carelessly for about ten minutes before she decided to go under once more. She dove under water, hitting her wounded arm on a branch sticking out just under the surface. The ragged branch tore into her wound, ripping off the bandage and tearing the wound deeper than it already was. She immediately came up out of the water, gasping and choking on the water she'd accidentally swallowed. As she went back down again in a pool of fresh blood, the guards jumped in after her. She fainted before they reached her, the pain suddenly intolerable. She slipped under water again just as the guards both reached her and brought her to the surface. They dragged her to shore and laid her on the sand. She was unconscious, but breathing.

"Lord Byron will surely hang us for this," said Christian, breathlessly. "Let us get her back to the cabin now; her wound is gushing blood." Christian picked her up carefully while Peter grabbed his tunic and ripped it, his muscles bulging out, and put the ripped piece tight against Gabrielle's wound.

They ran through the village with her lifeless body, the village people staring and shouting and running after them. Peter ran ahead and kicked in the door to Lord Byron's house, awakening the ladies. They jumped up when they saw Gabrielle. Christian laid her on the bed and started pressing down on the wound and mopping up the blood with fresh rags the townswomen were bringing in. Sasha, who was also known as the village doctor, hurried to apply some of the medicine which she always kept in a bag nearby, but was not sure it would do much good. Gabrielle was already slipping into a light coma from the blood she had lost; she was still losing blood and was not yet out of danger.

"We need Lord Byron, now," Sasha ordered.

Peter was first to speak up. "I will go. I will have him back by daylight." He left quickly and quietly, riding off swiftly into the night.

Gabrielle slept in a deep, deep sleep, dreaming of dangers, of her home, of Byron and his village. All night, Sasha, Maggie, Christian and a few other townsfolk took turns watching over her, afraid to speak out loud of the possibilities that lie before them.

CHAPTER 5

Peter rode as he had never ridden before. God forbid, if anything happened to the Princess, Lord Byron would surely have his head mounted on the wall. He could tell his Lord was in love with Gabrielle. He was never that way with the other ladies he brought home.

Peter had ridden for nearly two hours when he finally stopped. He was very good at hearing little things as he rode. He knew someone was in the bushes watching him.

"Show yourself!" he ordered as he got off his horse and drew his sword. Before he knew it, two burly men jumped on him from behind. They knocked his sword out of his hand. He knew he was a goner. Then he recognized one of the voices as Sebastian's.

"Wait! It is Peter! I come looking for Lord Byron!" They all let him up at once.

"Peter? What in God's name are you doing out here at this hour?" Sebastian asked incredulously.

A tall figure emerged from the shadows. "That is what I would like to know." Lord Byron said in a very stern, angry voice.

"It is the Princess, my Lord," Peter answered breathlessly. "You need to come back to the village, right now." He knew it was not his place to order the Lord to do anything, but this was a serious situation.

"Where is Gabrielle? What has happened?" Lord Byron asked as the men mounted up and prepared to leave.

"I will explain on the way, my Lord. Your lady is in danger; we need to ride hard."

The urgency he saw in Peter's face was enough to strike fear into Bryon's heart. Peter, like himself, was not a man who worried or feared much. Knowing there was not time to waste, Lord Byron jumped on his horse and they all started riding into the darkness.

An hour later, the men arrived back at the village. Having had the whole story explained to him en route, Lord Byron flew off his horse just as Sasha was running out of his cabin.

"My Lord, she has spiked a fever and I cannot get it down!" Lord Byron saw the raw fear in Sasha's eyes. His worst fears were coming true; things did not look good for Gabrielle.

Lord Byron ran to Gabrielle's bedside and took her hand. He uncovered her wound and assessed the damage: it was worse than he feared. *All this from a branch in the water?*, he wondered to himself. Gabrielle's face was pale and her breathing shallow. He realized that everyone was watching him and hollered for them to leave him alone. Sasha started to object but he barked at her even louder and she, too, quickly left him alone with the woman he loved.

Lord Byron tenderly looked at Gabrielle's beautiful face; she reminded him of a sleeping angel.

"Gabrielle, come back to me," he whispered, blinking back tears. "I promised your father I would take care of you, and look what I have done to you. I could not bear to be without you, my love. I know you have the strength in there. You have to fight it, girl! Get the poison out of you!" He could not stop the tears from falling as he bent down and kissed her lips. A few moments later, he wiped his eyes and went outside.

"Peter, Christian, take the men down to the lake. I want to be sure it was just a branch or something in the water that caused this, not anything or anyone else." He saw the surprise in their faces that he would think an intruder could be in his village, but they did as he asked and rode away quickly. Lord Byron went back inside to be with his dear Gabrielle. He rested only slightly better when the word came back that nothing but an old tree branch had been found in the depths of the lake water.

Gabrielle remained in a coma for another whole day, although the bleeding finally stopped and she started showing signs of improvement. Lord Byron decided not to alert the King yet, as the Princess was in stable condition and he felt she would pull through as strongly as ever. He only left her side when he was required to see to the most urgent business matters in town. He did not even sleep or eat for the two whole days she was out, in order to protect her.

On the third morning, Lord Byron was upstairs going through some belongings of his parents when he heard a noise behind him. He turned to see Gabrielle standing at the top of the stairs. He jumped to his feet and went to her, hugging her, making sure not to hurt her.

"What are you doing out of bed, Gabrielle?!" He asked as he gently picked her up and carried her back downstairs, straight to her bed. She tried to object, but did not have the strength. She looked worn and sick, and had obviously lost a lot of blood.

"What happened, Byron? Why do I feel as if I have been trampled by a dozen horses?"

"Hush, Gabrielle. You need your rest. You have been in a coma for just over two days. You had a little accident down by the lake and have lost a lot of blood. I thought I nearly lost you again"

Gabrielle could see the stern worry and tenderness in his eyes, all at the same time. She put her hand to his face to reassure him that she would be fine. Her touch felt so good to him. She was back with him -- he knew she would pull through. He kissed her hand and smiled. Then, an angry look came over his face.

"You had orders to stay right here, Gabrielle. You could have been killed. Your father was right about your stubbornness. You will stay here until you get better now, do you hear me? And I will be here by your side the whole time." He was standing with his hands on his hips, talking down to her, and Gabrielle couldn't help but chuckle at him.

Taken back by her reaction, he sat down on the edge of the bed and demanded to know why she was laughing at such a serious matter. Gabrielle put his face in her hands and pulled him to her, kissing him passionately. It took all of her strength, but she did not care. He was there with her, and that was all that mattered. Suddenly she fell into his chest and started sobbing. He wrapped his strong arms around her and held her. He knew she was in pain and the only thing that could help her now was time.

Sasha had sewed up her wound and was treating it every day to prevent infection again. After a long, seemingly endless night of waiting, Gabrielle's fever finally broke the next morning and she seemed to be regaining her strength. Lord Byron rejoiced as she came back to life; although she still faced a long recovery, he felt the worst of the ordeal was over and dared not to think what could happen if it happened again.

The next few days Gabrielle focused on making a strong, steady recovery. Sasha and Maggie were with her every morning, helping her to bathe, to dress and to do her hair.

One afternoon, she awoke from her nap. At first, she thought she was alone in the cabin, but as she turned to get out of bed, a giant hand grabbed her waist and pulled her back down. Lord Byron was lying right at her side and she had not even noticed. *My goodness*, she thought, *how ill have I been?*

"Good afternoon, my beautiful angel. How are we feeling today?" Lord Byron said before greeting her with a long, passionate kiss. She replied greedily, wanting him more than ever before.

"I feel great today, my Lord. Much better to see you here by my side."

"I have not left your side since my return, my Lady."

"Yes, I know. I also heard you have not slept nor eaten while I was ill. What do you mean by putting your own health at risk, Sire?"

Lord Byron rolled his eyes and dismissed Gabrielle's feeble attempt at scolding him. She knew he would survive without sleeping or eating and she could not convince him otherwise. He pulled her closer to him and dropped his hand down to her breasts, which were already swollen and erect. She smiled at him and kissed him long and hard, dropping her own hand to find his stiff muscle waiting for her touch.

She was pleased to find that he was already naked in bed with her, his skin warm all over, warming even more to her touch. Her nipples pressed against his chest, and his hard cock pressed against her wetness. It had been so long since she'd felt this way, she literally ached for more. He was careful not to touch her wounded arm, which was lying at her side.

He rolled her over so that he was straddling her. He could see the fire and passion in her eyes. She was ready and waiting for him. He entered her softly and gently, not wanting to cause her any more pain. She gasped at his stiffness, at his ease and at the raw feeling of pleasure that just entered her. She put her arm over his shoulder, pulling him down on top her, while her other hand clenched the sheets, her nails digging down into the mattress below.

He rocked her slowly, sinking in deep and withdrawing almost all the way out before going back in. She was in heaven. He leaned down and sucked on each of her nipples, causing her to throw her head back and arch her hips in ecstasy. When she did this, he moaned loudly. It drove him crazy when she did that, as it made him lose all control. He started pumping faster and faster, their bodies gliding together, their sweat mixing, making them both slippery and their bodies sail as one. He pounded her harder and harder, his moaning getting louder and hers getting higher.

"My Lord, please, I cannot do this anymore!!" she begged, for she was already exhausted, but he did not stop. He drove into her hard and in that moment, they both exploded. She drove her mouth into his shoulder and he stuffed his into the pillow, to muffle their cries so the townsfolk would not wonder what was going on. The spasms in Gabrielle's body made her cry. Her arm was throbbing, but so was everything else. Byron rolled off of her in time to see her wiping her tears.

"Have I hurt you?" He asked tenderly, a concerned look on his face.

"No, Byron, I am fine. The pain medication is just wearing off, that is all."

"I will get Sasha; she will attend to you then."

"No, please," Gabrielle insisted. "Stay with me here, and hold me." He did just that and they fell into a deep sleep together.

The next week together was blissful. They made love at least three times a day. When they were not doing that, they were out walking together, or doing exercises to strengthen Gabrielle's arm. She continued to recover at a rapid rate, and was feeling like herself again in no time. She found herself starting to love the little town, the people, and everything around her.

Lord Byron and Princess Gabrielle were walking through one of the flower gardens on one of the typical bright, sunny days, when Gabrielle paused and thoughtfully looked out into the garden. Byron could see something was on her mind.

"What is it, Gabrielle?"

"This is your home, Byron. The people here, they are so different than me. I would never fit in here if I were to stay with you. The people here, they seem like, well . . ."

"Savages?" Lord Byron lifted his eyebrows at her.

"Well, in a matter of speaking. I don't know what to call them! Oh, this is all so confusing. I want to be with you, but…"

"But what, Gabrielle? There is nothing to think about. Your father has already given me permission to have you. You will be my wife and stay here with me. What is there to think about?" In the back of his mind, Byron knew he was lying to her but he fully intended to ask the King for her hand and he knew in his heart that the King would oblige. Gabrielle's father loved him like a son, and would want nothing more than to have his daughter taken off his hands by his trusted friend Byron.

Gabrielle stared at him in disbelief. "How can you simply order me around like I am a child? I cannot believe how you can go from absolutely wonderful to so damn arrogant in less than a minute!"

"Do you deny that you love me?" Lord Byron responded.

"What does that matter? It --"

"Do you deny it?" he repeated a bit louder.

"Well, no, I don't," she answered humbly.

"See then, you love me, and there is nothing else to think about. If I asked you to stay here, you would say yes and be with me forever."

Lord Byron started walking away without her, leaving her to stand there with her jaw dropped. She wanted to yell and scream at him, but she knew he was right. She hated him for being right all the time, but she loved him all the same. *Damn him! Damn him for making me love him so much*, she thought to herself. Without another word, she quickly caught up with him, taking his arm, paying no attention to the smirk on his face.

CHAPTER 6

There were only a few days left until Gabrielle was to go back home, and she was not sure if she wanted to go back or not. Of course, her father was expecting her, but Byron was planning on asking the King for permission to make her his wife. It was all so confusing. She did want to marry Lord Byron, but who would take care of her father?

She was not feeling well that morning, running outside several times to throw up. She was growing pale and had the chills. Sasha and Maggie had been taking turns seeing to her, much to her dismay.

"This is nonsense," she grumbled as she slowly climbed back into bed again. "I have been nothing but trouble since I came here. I should go home and just not bother anyone anymore."

Sasha felt her forehead again; the fever seemed to be coming down, but the Princess was just as nauseous as ever. "You have been no trouble at all, my Lady," Sasha spoke soothingly. "You just need a little rest and you'll be back on your feet in no time; now stay here while I go and speak with the Lord."

Gabrielle watched quietly as Sasha put her water basin down and headed out to the village to find Lord Byron. The Princess had already decided that she just could not take it any longer; she had to get back to her father's and stop being such a burden to Lord Byron and his people. Her mind made up, she packed a few things and headed out the door, stopping to tell Peter, the guard, her intentions.

"Have you gone mad, my Lady?" Peter said with a dumbfounded look on his face. "Lord Byron will have you for lunch if he finds out!"

"I know he will be displeased, Peter," she reasoned. "But I have caused more than enough trouble, and he cannot possibly tend to his duties around here while worrying about me all the time. I am giving you an order to take me back to the King's castle at once, and I won't hear another word about it."

"Yes, my Lady," Peter replied obediently. "I shall see that you get home safely." In a few moments he had their horses ready to go, and gingerly helped the Princess mount up.

Unbeknownst to Gabrielle, Peter had also motioned for Christian to notify Lord Byron at once. As quickly and quietly as possible, Christian also mounted up and headed for the outskirts of the village where he believed Lord Byron was hunting, not realizing that the Lord was conducting business in town that day. As Christian set out through the woods, Peter and Gabrielle headed down the road for the day's ride that lay between them and her father's castle.

Meanwhile, Sasha arrived at the entrance of the tent where Lord Byron and his men were meeting. He had not been pleased with the recent change in Gabrielle's condition, but decided to let her sleep, agreeing with Sasha that the Princess simply needed some rest. Still, he could barely contain his worry and frustration as he listened to Sasha's most recent report.

"What is wrong with that girl?" he asked. "I hope she is not infected from her wounds again."

Sasha took a deep breath and stepped forward.

"May I speak freely, my Lord?" she asked as she knelt down in front of him.

He did not like the look on her face. "But of course, Sasha, what is it?"

Nothing could have prepared him for Sasha's next words. "I may be wrong, my Lord, but you know that I am often not. I believe that Princess Gabrielle might be…well…with child, my Lord."

"What?" Lord Byron gasped in shock. With child? *Pregnant*? But of course -- Gabrielle was carrying his baby! Now they would definitely have to get married, before her father found out. This was wonderful news!

"Does she know yet?" Lord Byron asked, thrilled at the idea of giving her the happy news himself. He knew very well that she would be outraged, of course, getting in such a state out of wedlock.

"No, Sire, I did not mention it to her."

"Good! Then no one must say a word. I will talk to her first to keep her calm. This is grand news, men!" he exclaimed, stopping to slap Sebastian on the back on his way out of the tent, as the other men offered cheers and congratulations to their Lord.

Lord Byron began walking happily toward his cabin. He was nearly home when Christian rode up to him frantically.

"Lord Byron, I have been looking for you for an hour, Sire!" He stopped to catch his breath, and Byron sensed something was terribly wrong.

"Spit it out, Christian!" Lord Byron said gruffly.

"It's Princess Gabrielle, my Lord. She has gone."

"Gone?! Gone *where*?" Lord Byron bellowed loudly and nearly pulled Christian off of his horse.

"She insisted that Peter take her back home to be with her father, Sire. They left but an hour ago. She was worried that she was causing you too much stress worrying about her."

Lord Byron was furious. He quickly mounted the horse and beckoned to his four head soldiers. "She thinks I was too *worried*? So she leaves with just *one* soldier, to cross dangerous grounds to get home? *And* she is carrying my child?! Why in the hell would I be worried!" he complained to no on in particular. Without another word, he spurred the horse and headed down the road out of town, his soldiers in tow, riding hard to catch his dear love before someone else could.

What Lord Byron knew, and was pretty sure Princess Gabrielle didn't, was that Lord Sherlton's men loved to prowl around the forest just before King Mathew's land. It was very dangerous territory for Gabrielle. Even though Peter was a giant soldier, there was no way he could take them on alone.

Gabrielle and Peter were riding steadily along when Gabrielle suddenly stopped and dismounted.

"Are you all right, my Lady?" Peter asked, dismounting as well while eyeing her closely.

"I am fine, thank you, Peter. I just need to rest a bit. I have an awful stitch in my side." Gabrielle walked over and sat on a tree stump while the horses grazed for a bit. Peter watched her protectively and knew that something was wrong with her; she was very sick.

"My Lady, if I might just give you an honest opinion, you are in no condition to be traveling out here in this heat. You are already weary with some kind of flu or something, and this heat is making you worse. You should be back at Lord Byron's home, resting and getting well, so that your father and our Lord won't have to worry about you."

Gabrielle knew he was right. Her father would curse her up and down for her taking off like that, and while she was sick on top of it. "I know, Peter. But I just hate to be such a pain. Look at me! Trouble is following me everywhere! I was shot, I wounded myself swimming, and now I have the flu! Your Lord has better things to do than worry about me and check on me all the time. There is only half a day's ride left to my father's castle; let us get on with it." She stood up to walk over to her horse when her head started spinning madly. She stumbled a bit, the world turning grey, and held her hand towards Peter.

"Peter! Peter, please help me, I feel --" she pleaded weakly just as she collapsed. Peter reached her just in time and caught her in his arms.

"My Lady!" Peter cried, but could not awaken her. She was right, he thought, trouble followed her everywhere. Royalty or not, he knew they were closer to the village than to the King's castle. He carefully laid her on her horse's back, climbing up behind her to hold her in place as they rode. Grabbing the reins in his hand while holding the fragile Princess tightly, he rode back to the village as hard as he could.

Lord Byron and his men had just passed the first clearing when he could see the two galloping horses approaching in the distance. Defensively, and fearing the worst, he jumped off his horse and immediately went for his sword. His men followed, prepared for battle. As the horses got closer, he could see that one was riderless and the other was carefully carrying a strong man and a lifeless-looking damsel. Byron's knees nearly went out from under him as he realized it was Peter and Gabrielle. *Please, let her be all right*, he pleaded silently. He put back his sword and ran to meet them.

"My Lord," Peter started, "she just collapsed. I was bringing her home to you." Lord Byron quickly took Gabrielle and laid her on the ground. She moved her head slowly and, just then, made a sound.

"Byron?" she whispered.

"Gabrielle, hush, we are going to take you back home." He picked her up and got on his horse, in one swift motion, as if she weighed nothing at all.

He did not need to say a word to his men. They had already mounted as well and soon were all headed back home.

Gabrielle awoke again and found herself in Byron's lap, on his horse. She started to wonder where exactly they were headed, when it came to her: they were in his village, heading for his house. She never even made it to her father's. She remembered sitting and talking to Peter, then she must have fainted, as awful as she was feeling. She looked up at Byron, who had a determined look on his face. They ran through the village and right up to his cabin, where Sasha and Maggie were patiently waiting.

"Byron, please," Gabrielle tried to argue as he helped her down to her feet. "You should have taken me back to my father. I will be fine."

"What were you thinking, taking off like that, Gabrielle?!" He was yelling at her now in front of everyone. She put her head down speechlessly, like a child being scolded. He grabbed hold of her chin and slowly picked it up and looked at her.

"You scared the life out of me, girl. In your state, you should not be out in this heat -- or riding a horse like mad, either!"

"In *what* state? I just have a little bug, and it will go away if everyone would just leave me be and stop fussing!" Gabrielle pushed his hand away and turned to go in the cabin.

"You don't have 'just a bug', Gabrielle," he called after her. The others caught on and walked away to give them some privacy. Gabrielle had already gone inside and was sitting on the side of the bed when Lord Byron sat next to her.

"Sasha is a great healer," he began explaining tenderly. "She has great knowledge in the ways of health and medicine. She came to me earlier to tell me that she believes you are pregnant – and I believe it as well." As he saw her face pale again, he was ready to catch her but, alas, she did not faint. She gasped and looked at him wide-eyed.

"What did you say? I am with child?"

"Yes, Gabrielle. You are carrying my child. Is that not wonderful news?" he beamed.

"Are you mad? What will my father say?!" She got up and started pacing the room. "He will be so ashamed of me! Oh, what have I done? I have become a harlot!" She sank to her knees next to Byron and cried into the bed.

"I don't want to hear you say that. It is simple; we will just get married and not tell your father about the baby until afterwards."

Gabrielle looked at him as if she had just been slapped. "And lie to my father? Have you completely lost your mind?"

"It won't be lying, Gabrielle. We just won't tell him yet. I will let it be your choice on whether to have a big wedding, or something simple."

Gabrielle stared off into the distance, the truth sinking in. The cards had been dealt; she had to get married now. She knew she would eventually marry Byron, but it was not supposed to happen like this, not at all.

CHAPTER 7

Gabrielle awoke to the sound of horses riding by the cabin. She yawned and stretched. Her hands instantly went to her belly, as if protecting her child from the unknown. She still could not believe she was carrying Byron's baby. She thought of all of the arguments they'd had and how many times they had made up so wonderfully. She smiled and slowly got out of bed.

Mornings were not her best just yet, with the waves of morning sickness rolling in. She steadied herself and went to get a drink of water. As she turned around to go sit back on the bed, her eyes wandered off to the side, toward the stairs. Byron had warned her not to go up there. What was he hiding that was so forbidden? If she was to be his wife, she had a right to know. She knew Byron was out training with the men that morning, so she quickly and quietly tip-toed up the stairs. Although there was no one else about, she felt as though she needed to be extra careful, since Byron forbade her to climb them.

It was dark and musty upstairs, like an old attic that had not been touched for days. There were boxes everywhere. At the end of the room, Gabrielle instantly spotted a very large trunk. Something drew her to this trunk. Something else told her not to open it, but her female intuition and raging pregnancy hormones got the best of her.

She knelt in front of it and rested her hands on top of it. What if it was something horrible that would cause her to hate Byron? What if it uncovered a ghastly secret that she would never want to know? The "what ifs" were nagging at her horribly; she shrugged them aside and slowly picked up the lid. It creaked, announcing that it had not been opened for a long time. Dust fell from every corner. She blew the dust away, coughing and sneezing. When the dust settled, she could only stare. Her stomach went into a huge knot as she stared at the contents of the box. She couldn't stop herself from reaching inside. She started breathing heavily and was about to stand up with a woman's gown in her hands when she fainted right there, vaguely aware that two giant hands grabbed her as she went down.

"Gabrielle. Wake up." Lord Byron knew it was just a fainting spell, so there was no sympathy in his voice. Gabrielle's eyes fluttered and slowly opened. She saw Byron sitting on the bed at her side. The look on his face was not a happy one. She closed her eyes for a minute and tried to remember what had happened. She remembered going upstairs; she must have fainted again. Then she remembered the trunk! Her eyes flew open and she gasped loudly. What exactly had she found in that trunk? Whatever it was, Byron was very displeased with her. She bolted upright in bed and tried to talk.

"Don't bother, Gabrielle. You deliberately disobeyed me! And for that you shall be punished," Byron said coldly. "I asked you -- no, I told you specifically to not go up to that room, and you did not listen! Do I have to treat you like a child, woman?!" Byron was up pacing the room now and all Gabrielle could do was sit there, dumbfounded.

"Excuse me? Did you just say that I was to be punished for not *listening* to you?" Gabrielle asked in disbelief. "Listen here, Lord Byron. I may be the mother of your child and your future wife, but it will be a cold day in hell before you punish me!" She was crying now, her hormones raging in full control.

"Don't talk to me like that, Gabrielle! You have got to get rid of that assinine stubborn attitude of yours, girl!"

Byron's words only set Gabrielle off into a more furious rage. "Don't you patronize me, Byron! I don't care that I disobeyed you! I don't care what you do to me, as long as it gets me away from you! Do you hear me? I don't want to live here! I don't want to be with you! Ever! I hate you! Now leave me alone so I can pack my things and go home to my father!"

Byron marched over to her side, grabbed her chin and lifted it up so Gabrielle had to look into his eyes. "You will be my wife, Gabrielle, if I have to drag you all the way to the altar. What on earth has gotten into you?"

Gabrielle pushed his hand away, not believing that he could not see why she was upset. "Are you for real? Are you that full of yourself that you don't even care why I am upset or care that I found out?"

"Found out what, Gabrielle? What on earth are you talking about now?" He was sick of her games and tired of going in circles. He looked exhausted.

"The other woman, Byron," she managed to choke out before sobbing uncontrollably. "The other woman -- *that* is what I'm talking about. That is what I found up there, the reason you did not want me to be up there. You were married once before, weren't you? There is another love in your life, and I will not be second, do you hear me?! I will not be second to you!" She sat back down hard on the bed and held her pillow. She could not talk anymore; she was almost too exhausted to cry. She lay back down and sobbed silently. Byron sat next to her and she tried to move away from him, but it was no use; he held her there.

"Gabrielle, that was something I wanted to share with you when the time was right – I didn't want you finding out about it like this. I wanted to tell you on my own time."

"When was that going to be, Byron? After you had married me, then you would decide to tell me, 'oh by the way, there is another woman in my life'?" Gabrielle was becoming hysterical again and Byron snapped. He stood up and looked her right in the eyes.

"Yes, Gabrielle, there was another woman in my life! I loved her! I loved her with all of my heart and soul! Does that make you happy now? You were right; there is another woman besides you! Let me enlighten you about my little secret. The woman I loved was going to be my wife, many years ago. She was brutally raped and murdered by a man called Lord Sherlton. And I have never forgiven myself for not saving her that day. I have spent these last few years of my life vowing revenge on her assailant, and I swore on her grave that before I died, the bastard who killed her would die first. Yes, Gabrielle, I loved her. But she is dead now. Those are her memories up there. You are my only love now, and I would kill for you if I had to. Don't you ever forget that." Byron turned and stormed out of the cabin and slammed the door, leaving Gabrielle pale and speechless. She had just made a complete ass out of herself and hurt the man she loved. She tried to get up but she was too exhausted. She rested her head on the pillow and cried herself into a deep sleep.

Hours later, Gabrielle awoke to a knocking on the door.

"Come in," she called, sitting up in bed. Christian and Del walked in, bowing courteously. "What can I do for you two?" she asked, surprised at the serious looks on their faces.

"My Lady, may we have a word?" Christian asked politely.

Gabrielle nodded, and the two men sat down in chairs across from her. Del started, "We heard you and Lord Byron this morning. He told you of Elizabeth."

Gabrielle put her head down, ashamed. "Was that her name?"

"My Lady, please do not be so hard on yourself," Del reasoned. "You did not know, and he should have told you. He never speaks of her."

"So it is true, then? She was the love of his life?"

"Yes, my Lady, she was," Christian said, "but you are now. Byron was not always a hard, stubborn ass like he is today. He was once the most generous, forgiving, kind-hearted person you'd ever know. But when he saw Elizabeth lying there that day, he realized he was helpless against saving her and something inside him snapped."

Gabrielle looked at both of them incredulously. "So he has been carrying this rage around with him for all these years?"

"Yes, my Lady. But he loves you now. You are his future. Elizabeth is a memory. Our Lord will never go back to the way he was, but in time, his rage will die down and his soft side will show again."

"That is not what bothers me, Christian," Gabrielle said quietly. "I just wish I could help him forget and get rid of the pain.

Gabrielle looked down at her hands and Del came over and took them. "I think I know of a way."

Lord Byron threw another stone in the lake and sat back against the tree he had sat under so many times before. Why hadn't he just told Gabrielle about Elizabeth so it would not have come to this? *She will adjust*, he thought. Then his thoughts turned to Elizabeth. He still missed her, but she was part of his past; Gabrielle and their child were his future. He sighed and put his head in his hands.

"What was she like, Byron?"

Byron jumped at the sound of Gabrielle's voice. He stood up to greet her; she was breathtaking, as usual. She was in a pale yellow gown with his coat of arms on over her to keep her warmed from the chilling breeze coming off the lake. Her hair was tied back and little wisps were blowing gently around her face. She sat down next to him and pulled him back down, staring intently at him, waiting for an answer.

Byron cleared his throat. "She was a natural beauty, like you. Her hair was dark as chestnuts, thick and full. Her eyes twinkled, like yours do. They were bright green. She loved to smile. She loved to laugh." Byron looked off into the distance, remembering.

"I wish I could have met her, she sounds wonderful." Byron looked at his amazing Gabrielle sitting next to him; talking with him about a woman he loved years ago, a woman whose death he vowed to live his life avenging.

"You and Elizabeth would have gotten along just fine, Gabrielle. Elizabeth was like you in many other ways. She was kind and generous and wanted nothing more than for others to be happy. We were to be married, but fate did not see it that way. Elizabeth was meant to be one of God's Angels, Gabrielle, and she sent you to me. She wanted me to be happy and she sent you. I am so sorry for scaring you. I will get rid of all of those things if you want me to."

Byron had a single tear rolling down his face. Gabrielle was crying as well as she leaned in and kissed his face, kissing the teardrop away.

"No, Byron, you may keep them. If she was that important to you and she brought us together, then we will keep them."

Gabrielle and Byron sat together in an embrace for what seemed like forever, remember the past and looking out for the future.

CHAPTER 8

The next morning, Gabrielle felt nauseous as ever and with a splitting headache to boot. She tried to get up but the room starting spinning and she immediately sat back down. She looked around – Lord Byron was nowhere to be found. Sasha came in right away with her medication and some water.

"You must take this, my dear," she ordered. "It will calm down your nausea and help you relax." Gabrielle quietly took the medicine and lay back down. She felt just awful.

"Sasha, where is Byron?" she asked sleepily. Sasha looked down but avoided the Princess's eyes.

"He has, um, gone for a ride, my Lady," Sasha answered quickly, then curtsied and hurried from the room. Gabrielle thought she was acting strange, but nevertheless, she was too tired to ask questions and fell into a fitful sleep.

Lord Byron and his men rode hard that morning. They were up at dawn and rode straight to the edge of Lord Sherlton's lands, where his men were known to lurk, and waited. Soon enough, they ran across some of Sherlton's hooligans and caught one by surprise. Lord Byron, who was known and feared across the land for being merciless, jumped from his horse and grabbed him firmly by the collar.

"Where is Lord Sherlton?" Byron asked with fire in his eyes.

The soldier cowered underneath Byron's giant figure. "I...I don't know, Lord Byron. He left this morning and is not planning to return until tonight."

Byron grabbed him and picked him up so they were looking directly into each other's eyes. The soldier's face paled in fear.

"You tell that eel that I will be looking for him. I know those were his men that attacked my

Gabrielle, and I will be damned if he is going to live another day as long as I am near him!"

"Yes, sir. I will tell him," the soldier stammered. Byron dropped him to the ground with a hard thud and got back on his horse. His men all glared at the soldier on the ground and rode after Byron.

Rage was pulsing through Byron's head. It was known by many, with the exception of Gabrielle and her father, that Lord Sherlton had wanted Gabrielle for himself for quite some time. Byron couldn't believe he had the guts to hurt her when he was well aware that she now belonged to Byron. *Sherlton will pay for this*, Lord Byron thought to himself. *This time, I will get my revenge.*

Gabrielle woke with a start, escaping her bad dreams once again. She looked around and noticed no one else was around. It was nice to finally be alone. She got up slowly and stretched, realizing to her delight that she felt much better. Maybe a nice dip in the lake would refresh her a bit. *No diving this time*, she thought to herself as she grabbed a towel and headed out the door.

She did not recognize the two guards who were standing outside her door as she left. She was not alarmed, as there were many soldiers she had not met yet, but Byron always seemed to keep his most faithful men, like Peter and Christian, by her door. She dismissed the thought and started toward the lake. The guards smiled at each other mischievously and quickly followed.

"Where are you off to, Princess?" one of the guards called after her.

"Just going for a little swim, if you don't mind. I will be fine, you know. You really don't need to follow me." She kept walking despite their arguments.

"You know Lord Byron would never approve

of this, my Lady," he cautioned.

"I don't care right now; I need a bit of a refresher. I cannot possibly get hurt again!" she exclaimed gleefully. The guards dropped the subject, realizing it was pointless to argue with her.

They arrived at the lake and she decided to go swimming in her gown. Byron would surely have her head if he knew she swam in her undergarments in front of his men, not to mention what he would do to them for looking at his nearly naked and pregnant woman.

She walked out into the lake until the water was up to her waist and waved her arms around under the water. She decided to be brave and get the worst over with, holding her breath and ducking completely under the water. The water was very cold, and as she came up gasping, she suddenly felt two giant hands grab her arms, closing around her wound. She yelled out in pain and tried to turn around. Another hand went over her mouth and a bag was put over her head. She knew it was the two guards who followed her and was irate at the lengths they were going to keep her under control. Despite the searing, reawakened pain in her arm, she struggled and tried to get out of their grasp. It was no use; the two men easily out-powered the delicate Princess.

She was being dragged towards the water's edge, where she heard bushes moving and horses stomping impatiently. Then a voice she did not recognize spoke clearly: "Good job, men. Finally, I will have what I have been hunting all these years. Let's just see how long it takes for your precious loved ones to find you now, Princess Gabrielle. Where we are going, you won't have to worry about a thing."

He laughed a deep, throaty laugh. The two soldiers grabbed Gabrielle and threw her onto the horse, where the unknown man held her tightly. She was lying over his lap with her bottom facing up towards him.

"What a lovely view from up here," he sneered as he grabbed her soft, firm flesh. "We may even have to stop so that I might take advantage of the young, luscious Gabrielle!" She tried to squirm, but he kicked his heels into his horse and they turned and ran wildly into the woods.

Gabrielle's arm was throbbing and she couldn't stop crying. How she wanted Byron to come to her right now. Sasha had said he was out riding. What if no one noticed she was gone until it was too late? Fear started setting in and panic gripped her stomach.

They rode hard for a good hour and finally came to a stop. Gabrielle's stomach ached from lying in that position for so long. Her hands were bound together tightly, the rope already leaving marks in her tender skin.

Rough hands came up to her head and pulled away the bag. Gabrielle's face was pale and tear-streaked. The two soldiers were standing in front of her, sneering. They moved apart and another man stood between them, coming face to face with the bewildered Princess.

"Gabrielle," he said slowly, looking her over like she was a prize trophy. "Look at you, you've gone and made yourself all upset now. Allow me to introduce myself: I am Lord Sherlton."

He waited for a response, but she gave him none. Gabrielle stared daggers at him with a furious look on her face. He sighed deeply, and continued: "I am taking you away from those gargantuans that you call your friends, that barbarian you call your lover, to be with me. You can argue and fight all you like, but it will do you no good. You will not be seeing your father or your precious Byron ever again, so get used to it. If you whine and fight too much, I will simply give you a sound thrashing. I have beat women for less. We will take a break here and continue on. Have you anything to say?"

Gabrielle looked him right in the eyes. She was dead frightened but she would not let him see that. She forced herself to smile, then suddenly looked down and spat on his boots. Like a hair-trigger reaction, he backhanded her right across the face, knocking her onto the ground, showing her he meant business.

Her will to fight was gone, and she was exhausted and in excruciating pain. She stayed where she had landed on the ground and sobbed quietly, feeling defeated. She didn't want to think about what horrors awaited her with this Lord Sherlton -- she just wished Byron would hurry up and find her.

Unaware that anything was amiss, Byron rode peacefully through the village, immediately looking toward his cabin in hopes of catching a glimpse of Gabrielle. Alarm rose in his heart when he saw no guards outside the front door. He kicked his heels into his horse and raced to the cabin.

"Where in the hell are the men I put here?" he bellowed as he jumped off his horse. He threw open the door and his fears were confirmed -- Gabrielle was nowhere in sight. Maybe she went for one of her strolls, he tried telling himself. He hollered for Sasha and she came running.

"What is it, my Lord?"

"Where is Gabrielle?" When Sasha realized she was not in the cabin, she looked worried.

"She was in here a couple of hours ago. Christian was standing guard. She was sleeping, so I left her. I am so sorry, my Lord." She dropped her head in shame, and he dismissed her.

"Byron, look!" Sebastian yelled. He was

pointing to the ground just outside the door, where several sets of footprints went around and around, sliding this way and that. There had been a scuffle here. Off toward the side of the cabin, there were drops of blood. Byron drew his sword and walked to the side. The crimson drops led to a big bush. A pair of man's feet was sticking out from behind the bush.

Byron's heart sank, his stomach tied up in knots. Fearing the worst, he looked around the bush and his heart sank at what he saw. Christian lay unconscious on the ground, covered in blood. Byron reached down and felt for a pulse. He was still alive, but barely.

Lord Byron hollered back to the others, "Get over here and get him inside, now! Get Sasha over here to look after him! Round up every man with a weapon in this village. We are going hunting."

With Christian's care in the capable hands of Sasha and some of the other ladies, Lord Byron grabbed some villagers nearby and asked if they had seen Gabrielle. They said they had seen her going toward the lake with two guards in tow. Without wasting another moment, Byron jumped on his horse and raced towards the lake. Every man in the village rode after him, their swords drawn, ready to help in any way they could.

After seeing what the intruders had done to Christian, Lord Byron felt sick thinking about what might have happened to Gabrielle. He feared the worst. If anything happened to his Gabrielle, he did not know how he would go on.

Pushing those thoughts out of his mind, he rode on to the lake, hoping to find the Princess there. When they pulled their horses up, though, it was silent -- almost *too* silent. He looked around and saw they were alone. He looked on the ground and saw a set of hoof prints, then another; someone had recently been there, and the fresh hoof prints led off into the woods. Byron wheeled his horse around, hollered his command, and took off after them into the woods.

CHAPTER 9

Gabrielle had cried herself fast asleep in Lord Sherlton's bedroom. She had no idea where they were exactly, but the cabin she found herself in was much bigger than Byron's and a lot fancier.

Lord Sherlton stood in the doorway of the bedroom and watched her sleep. "Sleep now, my pretty thing, as you will need your rest to keep up with me later." He laughed a quiet, menacing laugh and walked out, leaving her sleeping alone in the large room. Then he turned around suddenly with a thought.

"What if Byron finds us? I doubt he will, but there is that chance. After all, he is a great tracker and hunter. Screw it, I will take her now!"

He walked over to the side of the bed and undressed himself. He was already hard just thinking about penetrating her, grinning from ear to ear at the thought of it. He grabbed her arm and with one harsh pull, rolled her over onto her back.

Gabrielle woke up startled. When she saw that Lord Sherlton was standing in front of her completely nude, fear rose in her face.

"What on earth are you doing?" she demanded. He laughed and pulled her down so her legs were hanging off the bed. Despite her tiring efforts to stop him, he grabbed her gown and ripped it from top to bottom, exposing her entire body.

"Let go of me!! I swear to you, Byron will have your head!!" She started screaming but soon paid for it when Lord Sherlton cracked her again on the face. He forced her legs open and rammed himself inside of her as hard as he could. Hot white lightning bolts of pain shot through Gabrielle, in her abdomen and in her groin. She tried to scream, but Lord Shelton's hand was held tightly over her mouth. He pounded her faster and faster, leaning down and biting her nipples hard enough to draw blood. She was crying hard now, not knowing how much longer she could take it. She felt a rip and could tell she was bleeding.

"Why, you're bleeding like a stuck pig, Gabrielle! Just like the spoiled little pig you are. Not anymore, girl!" He rammed her even harder and she passed out. He did not care, he kept going and going. On his face was a wild, evil grin. "What luck, Gabrielle, to finally have what I deserve."

Lord Sherlton's head jerked around when he heard the door fly open. In the doorway stood Lord Byron, larger than life, with a look on his face that would kill anyone. On his heels were all of his trusted knights, just as big and fearless as he was. Sherlton knew this was his very last moment.

Byron looked at Lord Sherlton, frozen in fear on top of his beloved, *in* his beloved. Blood was everywhere. Rage filled Byron's heart and soul. He let out a battle cry so loud, so blood-curling, his men even stepped back. The sound that came from his very soul was that of pure hatred, rage, and revenge mixed with pain and grief. It was the sound of fury. With one swift movement, like a ballet dancer, Byron had beheaded Lord Sherlton. All of the pain from the years before of his lost Elizabeth and the shock of seeing his Gabrielle lying there, all came out in that one swing, that one cry. The body fell lifelessly to the floor with a dull thud. He glanced at his men and they knew to continue the rest of the battle without him and they departed with battle cries just as loud.

Byron ran to Gabrielle's side, wiping the blood, covering her up, holding her in his arms. She moved and mumbled something and Byron's heart stopped. She was alive but barely. She opened her eyes and saw Byron. She let out a sigh of relief. Her pain was unbearable. Her hand moved slowly to her belly. They both knew the baby was lost. Byron held her tightly and cried with her for her loss, for their loss and for her pain. It seemed like hours had gone by before Byron let go of her. She looked at him with a soft tear stained face.

"I am so sorry Byr…"

He put a finger to her lips before she could finish. "There is no need to apologize for anything, my love. None of this is your fault. If any, it is mine for not protecting you better. It is I who should be apologizing. I swear on my father's deathbed, Gabrielle, no one will ever hurt you again." He held her tightly against his chest as she started crying again. Byron cried with her again, this time, for love. They knew then that they would be together always and nothing or no one would ever break that bond.

After cleaning her up, Byron gently lifted her in his arms and carried her down to his waiting men and the horses and they started on the long journey home.

CHAPTER 10

The weeks that followed were slow and painful for Gabrielle. Finding out about her baby and that she had lost it completely crushed her. She begged and pleaded with Byron not to go tell her father. She was still ashamed of what had happened and made Byron promise to keep it between him and his men.

Her arm wound had healed by now but the skin that had been torn down below still made walking painful. The bruises on her face healed within a week, during which she stayed in their cabin so no one could see how terrible she looked.

Byron never left her side. He sent Peter and Sebastian to King Mathew's to let him know that his daughter was a bit ill and would be staying with Byron for a couple more weeks. The King was actually delighted to have her out of his hair and was even more delighted that Byron and his daughter were spending so much time together.

Christian healed quickly as well, apologizing immensely every day for what happened, insisting that if he had been faster, maybe none of this would have happened. The guilt he felt was unbearable. Gabrielle assured him time and again that she did not blame him.

Gabrielle was taking a bath alone one day while Byron stood outside talking to the men. Del had been put in charge since Byron's every moment was with Gabrielle. Del looked at Byron and could tell he was thinking hard.

"What is on your mind, Byron?" he asked.

"Del, killing Sherlton was not enough. How can that simply be enough for what he did to her? After Gabrielle and I go back to her father's, we will leave the next day. I swear on my son's grave that every single one of his men will die by my hand."

Del was about to ask if that was really necessary, but by the look on Byron's face, he knew any argument would be futile. Byron would seek revenge until he and Gabrielle had no more pain.

Just then, Gabrielle came outside, looking as radiant as ever. She still walked a bit slowly at times, but all in all she was feeling a lot better.

"Are you ready to go, Byron?" She took his hand in hers and together they walked to the back of the cabin, in the yard, under a tree, where they had made a tiny grave for their unborn child. Gabrielle stood there and silently prayed while Byron, reminded of what Lord Sherlton had taken from them, just got even more furious. It was pointless for even Gabrielle to argue with him about this -- his rage was great and his mind was set.

That night they had a doctor come in from a nearby town to do an exam on Gabrielle, with Byron's watchful eye right there to see that he was only doing his exam, to see if she could still bear children. She was delighted when the good doctor told her yes she could and that she should be feeling better than ever in no time soon. When he left, Byron ran to her side and hugged her. They could have children. They were both equally delirious about the idea.

"Byron, let's have one right away!"

Byron looked at her oddly. "Are you sure? Before we get married, Gabrielle? What about your father? What about the emotional state you are still in after this ordeal?"

"We will get married this week! Oh Byron, I want to, please! It will keep my mind off of everything else if we have a nice wedding and a baby!! Please!!"

She was practically begging by now. Byron

laughed and could not refuse his beautiful woman.

"I swear to you Gabrielle, my love, not one soul will ever harm you ever ever again. I vow for the rest of my life I will protect you...and our children. Of course we can get married sweetheart, if that is what you want. And yes, we can have lots of kids if you want, too! Anything you like, sweetheart!"

Gabrielle's eyes flew open and she threw her arms around his neck. "Oh thank you Byron! You've just made me the happiest person in the whole world!!"

"Oh, I think I can compete with you for that title." He laughed heartily but it was interrupted by Gabrielle's passionate kisses. They embraced for what seemed like forever and went out to share the good news.

EPILOGUE

Two months later, everyone in the whole village and her fathers' kingdom were guests at one of the largest weddings they had ever seen. Gabrielle was two months pregnant with their first child. Though they wouldn't know for months whether it was a girl or a boy, they had names picked out already: for a girl, Annabelle, after her mother, and if it was a boy, it would be Christian Mathew. Christian cried when they told him.

King Mathew could not have been happier about the marriage and the new family. He invited them to live at the castle but they both refused, which actually made the King happy. He was delighted that his daughter had found her protector. She was his angel, and he was her guardian.

Standing at the altar, Gabrielle leaned over and whispered into Byron's ear. "What do you do when you finally realize that all of your dreams have come true?"

He looked down and kissed her on the lips lightly, then whispered back to her, "I don't know about you, but I'm going to spend the rest of my life making my wife the happiest woman in the world -- and then, of course, have fun making the seven children we are going to have." He grinned and winked at her, enjoying the shocked look on her face, as the priest was standing in ear's length of them.

Beaming with joy, they turned to face the crowd before them and finally profess their eternal vows to each other.

THE END

www.ingramcontent.com/pod-product-compliance
Lightning Source LLC
Chambersburg PA
CBHW051932240626
47153CB00004B/1463